51213884

CW01208323

DERBY CITY COUNCIL
WITHDRAWN FROM STOCK

No Late Fee Collection

This book is part of our No Late Fee Collection. We will renew it automatically for up to six months so there will be no late fees. Please return the book within six months or, if you want to keep it longer, please renew it.

You can renew in person, online or by phone.

www.derby.gov.uk/libraries

Renewal Line: 01332 641700

Dan's Dinner
Text copyright © Margaret Adams 2010
Illustrations copyright © Ian Bobb 2010
Edited by Catherine White

First published and distributed in 2010 by Gatehouse Media Limited

ISBN: 978-1-84231-064-9

British Library Cataloguing-in-Publication Data:
A catalogue record for this book is available from the British Library

Derby City Libraries Supply Unit	
51213884 8	
Askews & Holts	26-Oct-2015
A	£4.95
4810346	

No part of this publication may be reproduced in any form or by any means, electronic, mechanical, photocopying, recording or otherwise, without the prior written consent of the publishers.

Gatehouse Media Limited provides an opportunity for writers to express their thoughts and feelings on aspects of their lives. The views expressed are not necessarily those of the publishers.

Author's Thanks

I wish to thank my family for their support and my students for reading my stories!

Chapter 1 - Daniel

Dan stood by his cooker.

He had a cook book in front of him.

He was cooking dinner.

He took a quick look to make sure the dinner was not burning.

He stirred the pan.
It had been a long day at work
in the supermarket.
He was tired.
His feet were sore.

Dan moved from one sore foot to the other.
He was thinking.
He knew that everybody at work liked him.
He had worked at the supermarket
for just over five years.
Everybody there knew
he was a really nice bloke.

They knew that he did not say a lot.
He kept himself to himself.
They knew he did not say much about himself
so nobody knew him very well.
Still, they were sure
he was a good bloke.

Dan took the wooden spoon
and stirred the dinner again.
He was thinking about his past.

He was not from England.
He was from a country in Africa.
His family had always called him Daniel.
He was named after Daniel in the Lions' Den,
the bloke in the Bible.

He had only left Africa
after the bad thing had happened.
He had liked it there.
It was warmer than here.
He always seemed to feel cold here.

Chapter 2 - At home

At home in Africa,
he had not worked in a shop.
He had lived in a village with his family -
his old mother, his wife and his four children.

The children were so funny -
three boys and a little girl.
They had had a piece of land next to a brook.
They grew most of the food that they ate.
They had been good at it
and had even been able to sell some.

His mother loved to grow flowers.
Dan had thought it was a waste of land
but he had let her do it anyway.
It was not an easy life
but a happy one.

He had loved to walk around his land
in the early evening,
with his old black dog
running along beside him.
It was the time of day
when it was cooling down.
It was warm but not too warm.

He loved to watch the sun go down
and he loved to see the lovely colours
of the African sky.
He missed it here in England.
He missed a lot of things.

He stirred his dinner while he remembered.

Chapter 3 - Going to market

One day, Dan thought he would go to market to sell some of the food they had grown.
He had eaten his breakfast.
He got out his old bike.
It was broken so he had to fix the brakes before he went.

His wife made brooches
out of beads and pebbles.
She asked him to sell some brooches too.

She gave him some bread and some broth
for his lunch.
She kissed him goodbye.
He remembered all the years before
when she had been his bride.
He did not know he would not see her again.

It was a bright, sunny day.
A gentle breeze blew.
He had lots to sell - broccoli, beans, cabbages,
brooches and bracelets.
He was looking forward
to bringing the money back home later.

He rode over the bridge to the market.
It had been a long trip.

He was breathing hard when he got there.
He brushed the dust off his clothes.
He found a place in the corner
where he could sell his things.

He heard a man come running
into the market.
He was covered in blood and bruises.
Dan heard him shout,
"Trouble on the other side of the bridge.
Big trouble on the other side of the bridge."

Chapter 4 - The bad thing

A lot of what happened next was a blank.
He had blotted many things from his mind.
He remembered some things
but not everything.
He had jumped on his bike to get home.
He had been stopped at the bridge
by soldiers.
He remembered their uniforms -
blazers all dusty
from the dry mud on the road.
They would not let him go home
but they told him what had happened.

Men had come from a rebel army.
They had gone to his village.
They had used blades and guns.
They had killed everyone in the village.

His mother was gone.

His wife was gone.

His children were gone.

They told him this was a road block.

He should not go to the village.

There was a lot of blood.

It was too bleak for him to go.

Dan had stood under the blazing sun.
He heard what the soldiers told him.
He blinked back tears.
He was angry.
He was sad.
He was afraid.

He had blamed everyone.
He blamed the rebel army.
He blamed the soldiers
for not getting there in time.
He blamed God.
He blamed himself for going to market.

It was a terrible time.
After a while, he had come to Britain.

But today something had happened.

Chapter 5 - The visitor

Dan checked that the dinner was not burning.
It was nearly ready.

Today had started like any other day.
Dan had gone to work at Asco Supermarket.
He had worked in the shop for five years now.
Most of the time,
he put the tins out on the shelves.
Sometimes, he helped cut up the cheese
and put it out for the shoppers.
He liked cheddar cheese
and sometimes he would pinch a bit,
if no-one was looking.

He had been on an early shift at work today.
He had started work early.
He had got dressed
in his work shirt and trousers.
He had been at work since 6.30 a.m.

It was just before lunch
when Mary came to find him.
Mary was a charming woman, he thought.
She worked on the check-out.
She was quite short with a shrill voice
but he liked her.
She was married
and Dan thought she was not happy.
She did not have any children.

"Dan," said Mary,
"there is a young man to see you.
He says his name is Charlie.
He says he is your son."

Chapter 6 - Dinner

Dan had been very shocked
when Mary spoke.
She could see it in his face.
She got a chair.
Dan would not sit down.
He leaned on the chair.
He could feel a pain in his chest.

After a few minutes, he spoke.
"Is this some kind of cheap joke?" he asked.

Mary took Dan into the shop.
A young man stood by the shelves
where they kept the shampoo.
Dan looked at the young man.
The young man looked at Dan.

"Dad," he said. His voice shook.
Then he smiled.
That was when Dan knew it was true.
It was Charlie.
He knew that cheeky smile.
Charlie did not look the same
but his smile was the same.
He had always had a smile like sunshine.
He still had.

Charlie told Dan about the day the men came.

Charlie had seen terrible things.

They had made him go with them.

He had done terrible things.

He did not choose to do them.

They made him.

But now he had escaped.

A charity had helped him find his father.

Dan stood back from the cooker.
He checked the dinner – chicken and chips.
They had cherry pie for dessert.
It was all ready.

He and Charlie had a lot of catching up to do.
They sat down at the table together.

THE END

A comprehensive set of tutor resources, mapped to the Adult Literacy Core Curriculum, is available to support this book:

Dan's Dinner Tutor Resources CD-Rom
ISBN: 978-1-84231-065-6

Author's Note

I have written short stories for individual students on quite a few different occasions, usually to help them practise a particular letter pattern, consonant blend, digraph etc., or to meet an observed need of the particular student.

Dan's Dinner is the third title in the Supermarket Stories series. It was originally written for students within English Workshop, a literacy class within the ACRES consortium in East Sussex.

The main intention of the series is to give Entry level students a story to read. I have often found that books for students at this level don't always have a story as such, and, as someone who enjoys stories, I wanted to give my students the same opportunity. I wanted to show that reading can be a pleasure, not just a necessity.

They are adult stories with adult themes. I have written them so that students can read a chapter per session and I have finished each chapter at a point that will encourage the reader to come back for more.

Each chapter can be used to practise specific learning aims, although this does not have to be the case. The supporting resources also check comprehension and encourage the reader to think more broadly about the text. I hope that this will encourage the reader to see the relevance of reading stories - *they make you think, not just read.*

Margaret Adams

If you have enjoyed this book, why not try one of these other titles from Gatehouse Books:

Pam's Secret　　　　　　　ISBN: 978-1-84231-050-2
by Margaret Adams

The first book in the Supermarket Series. Pam shares a secret with Jenny, her new friend at work. Will Jenny betray Pam's trust?

Bob's Problem　　　　　　　ISBN: 978-1-84231-056-4
by Margaret Adams

The second book in the Supermarket Series. Bob likes his job on the dairy counter, but his boss has other plans for him. Bob is forced to reveal his problem. Then one day, a shocking event puts Bob's life on the line.

Life On The Buses　　　　　ISBN: 978-1-84231-025-0
by Eric Newsham

'Life on the buses. What fun! The best job I ever had in my life.' Read about some of the fun and antics Eric gets up to with his driver mate.

Getting Better　　　　　　　ISBN: 978-1-84231-026-7
by Marie McNamara

Marie's desire to improve herself is driven by the desperate wish to give her children a better start in life. *Getting Better* is an inspiring read.

Gatehouse Books®

Gatehouse Books are written for older teenagers and adults who are developing their basic reading and writing or English language skills.

The format of our books is clear and uncluttered.
The language is familiar and the text is often line-broken, so that each line ends at a natural pause.

Gatehouse Books are widely used within Adult Basic Education throughout the English speaking world. They are also a valuable resource within the Prison Education Service and Probation Services, Social Services and secondary schools - both in basic skills and ESOL teaching situations.

Catalogue available

Gatehouse Media Limited
PO Box 965
Warrington
WA4 9DE

Tel/Fax: 01925 267778
E-mail: info@gatehousebooks.com
Website: www.gatehousebooks.com